Twisted

Elise Noble

Published by Undercover Publishing Limited

Copyright © 2015 Elise Noble

All rights reserved.

ISBN: 978-1-910954-08-9

Edited by Charles Thomas

www.undercover-publishing.com

www.elise-noble.com

TRICK AND TREAT

"ARE THESE FANGS straight?" Bree asked, gnashing her teeth together.

Megan studied her friend as she put the final touches to her Halloween costume. "I think so. You probably need a little more blood on the left-hand side of your chin, though."

"Thanks, I'll be back in a sec." She headed for the bathroom where the mirror was located.

While Bree went to paste more of the mixture they had carefully concocted out of food colouring and corn syrup onto her face, Megan touched the side of her nose. Yes, the fake wart she'd stuck on there half an hour earlier was still there. She straightened up her witch's hat and swirled her cape around her shoulders. She was ready to go.

At Joe's house on the corner, Bree and Megan met up with more of their friends. As well as a vampire and a witch, their little group consisted of a pumpkin, a zombie and a skeleton.

"Where's Juno?" asked the pumpkin, who was actually called Rebecca.

"Don't know," said Steve, the skeleton. "I didn't see her at school today."

"Maybe she's sick," suggested Joe, adjusting his tattered sweater and stumbling around. "What do you think of my zombie walk?"

"Or just chicken," said Steve, as he walked around the room flapping his arms and making chicken noises.

"Well, whatever, she's late," said Bree. "We're not hanging around to wait for her. She knew what time we were leaving. No way am I missing out on the best night of the year because she can't get her act together."

Megan had only lived in town for a few months and barely knew Juno. They shared one class together, English, and the other girl hadn't gone out of her way to be friendly. While she felt a bit sorry that Juno was missing out on the Halloween celebrations, she could see Bree's point.

As the group filed out of the door, Megan clutched the cute bag her father had bought for her to put her haul in. She loved the cat embroidered on the side, with green sequins for its eyes. Her dad had really stepped up to the plate since her mother died the year before. He'd also been cool about her staying out tonight, and Megan was determined to take advantage of that.

Their first task was trick or treating, with the aim, according to the boys, being to eat enough candy to make yourself sick.

"What if people don't want to give us stuff?" Megan asked. "We're not actually going to play tricks on them, are we?"

"Sure, we've got a box of eggs just in case," Steve laughed. "We won't need them, though. Everyone always keeps a dish of candy by the door."

Within an hour, Megan realised Steve was right. Her bag was stuffed to bursting and her arm hurt a little from carrying it. She swapped it to her other hand.

"Having fun?" Bree asked.

Megan nodded enthusiastically. In the village she used to live in, only a handful of people bothered to dress up and go out. Most householders wouldn't open their doors, and she'd been lucky if her count of chocolate bars got into double figures.

And, according to Bree, there was more to come.

"Tell me about this House of Horror thing again?" Megan said to her.

Steve jumped in first. "Every year, old man Lucky opens up his house to the neighbourhood. He used to be a special effects designer in Hollywood, and he does it all out with monsters and bodies and stuff. It's awesome."

"It's a little creepy." Rebecca gave a shudder. "Everything's so realistic."

"Yeah, last year, he had this dead girl face down in the bath. The water was all red with her blood. Wonder what he'll have this year?" Joe asked.

Megan wasn't sure it was really her thing, but after Steve's chicken comments earlier, she didn't want the others to make fun of her if she cried off going.

The walk to Mr. Lucky's house took almost twenty minutes, and it seemed like everybody in town was headed out there. In between the streetlights, torch beams played over the grass by the side of the road as ghosts and ghouls, and witches and werewolves tramped along.

The house itself was large and imposing, a grey stone affair that would make the perfect setting for a horror movie. Behind it, shadowy woods rose up and formed a ghost's playground. Megan would rather give up her entire shoe collection than set foot in there.

Bree read Megan's mind. "They say they're haunted," she said, gesturing at the trees. "The ghosts of the bodies buried there come to life under a full moon to search for their killer."

Steve snuck up behind Bree and tapped her on the neck. She let out a little scream, then thumped him on the arm. "Don't do that!"

"Aw, scaredy cat?"

"Shut up."

"You know that's all made up, right?"

"Whatever." She pouted and gave him the cold shoulder.

Candles flickering inside carved pumpkins lined the driveway, each face more grotesque than the last. Who carved them? Someone skilled with a knife, that was for sure. The overhanging branches rustled eerily in the light breeze as the gang traipsed along beneath them. Megan shivered and crept closer to the boys, hoping they didn't notice and laugh at her.

The front door lay open, a dim light spilling out over the stone steps. Megan approached it with trepidation, but when she heard the whoops and hollers coming from inside, she relaxed a little. Those people sounded as if they were having fun.

The door was propped open by a monkey with a bolt through its neck. Its red eyes glared malevolently.

"All right! Frankenmonkey!" Steve laughed, patting it on the head.

Blood-red velvet ropes formed a walkway through the house. Small signs saying "Please do not touch the exhibits" were clipped on at intervals.

Why would anyone want to touch those, Megan thought. The small boy holding his own head was particularly gruesome. A row of eyeballs lined up on a shelf seemed to watch as she and her friends walked from room to room. Megan felt bile rise up in her throat at some of the scenes. Whoever came up with these ideas sure had a warped mind.

In the hallway, a pale faced young girl hung twisting from the bannister. Her left hand clawed at the rope around her neck, but her eyes were white lifeless, glazed over as they stared at a scene she'd never see.

On the counter in the kitchen, a severed hand chopped up a cucumber, and a package labelled "human brain" sat ready and waiting by a cauldron of soup. A dark haired lady leaned over the table, blood from two puncture wounds in her neck dripping into a wine glass, her face screwed up in pain.

"If Dracula did restaurants," Steve muttered as Megan backed into him.

Things got no better in the lounge. Megan's stomach churned at the sight of a girl laying face down on the couch, her head lolling at an unnatural angle. A mother-of-pearl handled knife stuck out from the middle of her back.

One of the most innocuous of scenes, perhaps, but it struck a nerve with Megan. Maybe it was because the victim seemed so young? Something about her reminded Megan of her own mortality, and she hurried to get out of the room.

On the way into the corridor, she bumped into a tall, thin man dressed as the Devil. Horns stuck out from his forehead, attached so skilfully she couldn't see the join. A forked tail hung from under his black and red tuxedo and his red contact lenses made her own eyes go funny.

Megan tripped over her own feet and fell into Steve again. He caught her with one arm and looked up at the Devil.

"Mr. Lucky, how you doing? This place is the shit!"

"I'm glad you like it, young man. It gives me great pleasure to do this each year." He looked across and focused on Megan. "And you, young lady, what are your thoughts?"

She gulped and forced herself to look at him. "I-I-It's a little scary."

He chuckled. "The dark makes it seem so." He leaned down, and spoke into her ear, "If you would like, next year you could come by earlier and I could show your my creation process."

His breath in her ear sounded like the whistle of the wind through the headstones in the cemetery where her mother was buried. A single word popped into her head, spoken in the soft voice she last heard in the hospital, just before her mother passed on: "Don't."

Lucky had her locked in his gaze. "I-I-I'll think about it," she got out, before she managed to break away.

He gave her a chilling smile. "I'd like that."

Megan scurried past him. Steve paused, and Megan heard him ask, "How do you get the smell in here?"

Was he talking about that faint metallic tang?

"It's a trade secret."

Megan moved out of earshot. The sound of the old man's voice felt like ants scurrying down her ear canal.

After a quick glance over her shoulder to check Steve was following, she hurried through the rest of the house. Fortunately Bree didn't seem to want to hang around, either. Although she'd seemed enthusiastic earlier, Megan sensed it was more of a show for the boys.

In the bathroom, Joe said, "The girl's not in the tub this year. Shame."

Megan peeked in. Instead of a body, there was a swarm of cockroaches rising from the plug hole.

"Yuck!" said Bree, leaning over for a look beside her.

Megan tried to block out the images of the rest of the house, but even so, she was still shivering uncontrollably by the time they got outside.

"Scared?" asked Steve.

"Just cold," she said.

He took off his jacket and put it round her shoulders. Maybe he wasn't such an ass after all.

"What did you really think? You looked white in there."

"Creepy. Although the worst bit was old man Lucky himself."

"I'll give you that. He looked like a freak in that Devil getup, didn't he? Don't worry, though. He's harmless."

***

Stan Lucky finally closed the front door after the last of his guests. He glanced at the clock. It had just gone midnight, and he used a hand to cover his mouth as he yawned. His mother taught him he must always be polite.

It had been a long day. He'd been up before dawn to get the house ready. No matter how much he tried to prepare in advance, there was always more left to do than anticipated and he wasn't getting any younger.

He went through to the kitchen and moved the severed hand so he could make himself a cup of coffee using the ridiculously expensive machine an over zealous shop assistant talked him into buying. He had one small, but very important, job left to do tonight and he needed to stay awake.

Once he felt the caffeine flowing through his veins, he made his way back to the lounge. The sheet of polythene was under the couch, just where he left it. He slid it out and carefully spread it over the carpet. Blood spots were a bitch to get out.

His knees cracked as he crouched down next to the body of the young girl and ran his fingers through her silky hair. *So delicate, like the breeze on a summer's day.*

The knife stuck for a second and he had to twist it gently as he pulled it out of her back. She landed with a bit of a thump as he rolled her onto the plastic and Stan winced. Even in death, she was still beautiful, but it was a good thing his little gathering had ended when it did because blood was starting to pool in her extremities. Purple wasn't her colour.

With regret, he lifted a finger to a scratch on her cheek. She'd struggled, that one. Feisty. What had she called herself? Jane? Julie? Something liked that. Stan couldn't quite remember.

No matter. She didn't need her name any more.

Stan rolled her up in the plastic, careful not to smear any blood in his home. Then he hefted her over his shoulder and carried her out to a waiting wheelbarrow.

As he took her on her final journey through the

woods, he thought back to what his father had told him. "Always good to hide things in plain sight, Stan, my boy." Of course, he'd been talking about decanting his vodka into a water bottle rather than bodies, but Stan had taken it to heart. And he loved the annual trick he played on his guests, too drunk or too stupid to notice.

After a brief trip through the woods, Stan upended the wheelbarrow and tipped the girl into her waiting grave. As he picked up the shovel to fill in the hole, he felt a twinge in his back.

"Maybe I'm getting too old for this," he mused to the empty air.

But as he walked back to his house, he knew he'd return next year. It was his little treat.

BAD REVIEW

I GUESSED THE entire plot in the first chapter and a child's picture book has more character development.

Cutting my toenails is more exciting than reading this book.

Brenda looked away from the screen and rubbed her eyes, praying that if she did it hard enough, the reviews would disappear. But it was no good. They still taunted her in all their "purchase verified" glory.

One star. If I'd made it to the end, I'd probably deduct that as well.

The hero had the charisma of a potato and I wanted to shake the heroine until her teeth rattled.

One star. One star. One star. One star. A solitary five star review, but it was clear from the comments the reader had got A Summer Symphony mixed up with a different book.

Amazon, Goodreads, iBooks, Barnes and Noble - it was the same everywhere. Readers simply didn't understand Brenda's new book. *There was no happily ever after*, one blogger complained. Well, of course not. A Summer Symphony was the story of one woman's quest to find herself, not another insipid romance.

These people were too short-sighted to understand great literature. But she, under the pen name Kristi Badger, had studied her craft for years. Kristi was a

New York Times best-selling author, for crying out loud. She may only have made the list for a single week back in 2002, but her words had earned her the right to be there. After all, the plagiarism suit that followed got thrown out of court.

But now this. How would she face the other members of her writing group this evening? The launch of her ninth book was supposed to be her big day. She'd organised for the pub landlord to put on a buffet and ordered a huge pile of paperbacks to sell.

How could she rectify the problem? Brenda made herself a nice cup of tea and paced the lounge as she pondered, stepping round the two boxes of bookmarks and the case of fridge magnets she'd had printed for her anticipated book signings.

She needed to balance the reviews out. That would help. She needed those little gold stars like Donald Trump needed a new hairstylist. One by one, she logged on to her sock-puppet accounts and posted comments that were a little more balanced. It only took an hour, and she smiled in satisfaction as she hit "post" on the last one. Her Goodreads average was up to 3.5 now.

Just for good measure, she loaded up Twitter and sent a bunch of "Buy this best-selling book" tweets out to the seventy-eight thousand followers she'd purchased. Numbers liked that always looked impressive, and it may not be a best-selling book yet, but it would be soon. She was certain of it.

There was just time for a trip to her hairdresser before her little soirée. At forty-seven, she needed a little help with her roots, now the grey hairs were starting to show, and she needed to look her best for when the reporter from the local paper showed up. She'd invited him personally when she "accidentally" bumped into him coming out of the newspaper offices the previous week. He'd promised to come and take a few pictures, and that made the hour's wait in the cold November drizzle worth it.

As she prepared to leave, Brenda couldn't resist checking her Amazon page one last time. What was that? A new review? Two stars.

The summer referenced in the title is clearly a British one, because the book is as dull and grey as the weather.

Brenda thumped the keyboard in frustration, and the escape key flew off and landed in a dusty corner. She was about to turn the monitor off when she spotted the name of the reviewer: Happy Reads Book Blog.

That two-faced bitch! Kerry "Happy" Fowler was in her book group, and always wittered on about the importance of honesty in the review on process, the sanctimonious bitch. As Brenda recalled, Kerry hadn't been keen on A Summer Symphony at their monthly critique circle. She said Brenda used too much purple prose. Kerry knew nothing. Setting the scene was an importance most novelists overlooked. Readers needed to be able to picture every scene exactly and feel the emotion.

Kerry wouldn't be so bloody happy when her new self-help book came out, Brenda would make sure of that.

***

At six o'clock, she dressed in her new twin set and

drove the half mile to the Fox and Pheasant. The landlord let them have the meeting room there for free every Tuesday evening as long as they bought a couple of bottles of wine. And after the day she'd had, Brenda needed a glass or two.

Half a dozen of her fellow bibliophiles were ensconced by the bar by the time she arrived, lugging a box of signed copies.

Doug leapt off his stool. "Here, let me get that." He hefted the box in his arms. "Shall we head upstairs?"

"Ooh, that sounds so naughty," Mary giggled.

The buffet was already set out on the table when they walked in, and Brenda resisted the urge to rip off the cling film and stuff herself silly with sausage rolls. She'd barely eaten that day in anticipation of the photos, and her slimming pants dug into her thighs.

Then came the question she'd been waiting all day for.

"So, how's the book launch going?" Mary asked. Six faces stared at her, waiting for an answer.

She took a slug of the wine she'd hastily grabbed from the barman on her way up. "I've been extremely pleased with it."

"How many copies have you sold?" the landlord asked as he bustled in with a tray of mini scotch eggs.

What business of it was his? Brenda didn't ask how much he earned, did she? She forced out an answer through gritted teeth. "I'm nicely into triple figures."

A hundred and one copies, to be precise. And she'd bought twenty-seven of those herself to give the rankings a little helping hand.

"That's fabulous!" Mary squealed, ignoring Brenda's scowl as she helped herself to an egg and cress sandwich. "I'm really nervous about publishing my own book. I mean, my beta readers all loved it, and so did my agent, but you never can tell, can you?"

No, you couldn't. Brenda's own agent declined to renew their contract, citing creative differences. He'd wanted her to change the entire ending of the story! Moron.

Thanks to the self-publishing revolution, Brenda had been able to perfect the novel to her own standards. She'd agonised over every sentence, every word, every nuance. Not that her beta readers had appreciated it. They'd been too blinkered to understand her creative vision.

"Publishing is never easy, but I've had a lot of practice now. And if you leave me a nice review, I'd be happy to help you out with your own launch."

"Er, okay."

Footsteps sounded on the stairs as a handful more people arrived. Melanie rushed through the door first, beaming from ear to ear.

"Saw your book on Goodreads, Brenda. It didn't look so good earlier but things certainly picked up this afternoon."

Brenda forced a chuckle. "The trolls were out in force this morning. Some people like nothing more than the downfall of a successful author."

"Exactly. I got an awful review once. Someone said there was too much sex in my book." She let out a peal of laughter. "You'd think the half-naked man on the cover would have been a giveaway."

Brenda suppressed a shudder. Melanie was one of those awful new breed of erotica writers - all sex and no story. Brenda wasn't sure what appalled her more - the people wrote the stuff or the droves that bought it. Still, Melanie hit number one on Amazon two months ago so she had to at least pretend to like her. "Some people should stick to comic books."

A few more people arrived, and Brenda searched through them for the reporter. Where was he? Clearly the imbecile had no concept of timekeeping. Kerry Fowler had the nerve to show up, though. Brenda resisted the urge to stuff a handful of cocktail sausages down her throat and reached for the wine again. A good red cured everything.

Everything except frustration. By the end of the evening, her fellow club members had hoovered up the canapés but only bought nine copies of A Summer Symphony. She recalled the apologetic look on Brian's face as he patted her on the shoulder.

"Not my kind of book, love," he said, glancing over at Kerry as he spoke.

What had the bitch said? Had she told Brian what she thought of Brenda's book? Was that the real reason he didn't want it? Brenda had a copy of his awful travel memoir that she used as a coaster, so the least he could do was buy one of hers in return. And the bloody reporter didn't turn up, either. Brenda had a good mind to email his boss.

Bubbling with anger, she almost broke an ankle as she stumbled out to her car with a box half-full of books. She considered calling a cab home, but she'd only had a glass or three. Maybe four. She'd be fine.

After three attempts, she got the key in the ignition and started the engine. Her Nissan Micra sputtered to life. As she steered down the road, windscreen wipers on, little yellow stars floated in her vision. She lived for those stars. Why couldn't the world accept her work for the masterpiece it was?

The world... and Kerry. Brenda spied her ahead, hurrying along the pavement with her hood up. The smiley logo of the Happy Reads blog flashed through her mind. Two stars? Two fingers, more like. A smile crept across Brenda's face as she spied the large puddle Kerry was walking past. A little adjustment to the left, and she'd soak her.

Poetic justice.

At exactly the right moment, Brenda jerked the wheel. There was a bump as the tyre hit the kerb, and Kerry's shocked face hit the windscreen right in front of Brenda's nose. Blood spattered across the windscreen, and the car bounced higher as it ran over Kerry's body then continued its bumpy ride down the slope into the woods. Brenda laughed the whole way to the bottom, the sound echoing in the darkness. Let's see if Kerry dared to give anyone a bad review again. Let's just see...

MISTRESS OF HER OWN DESTINY

WHY WAS MUSIC so loud at parties? Susan longed, just for once, to be able to hold a conversation at a normal volume. Instead, she stood back while a business acquaintance of her husband yelled small talk, trying to avoid being hit by flying spit.

"So are you going to the golf tournament next week?" he wanted to know.

"I believe so." Of course she was. The country club's annual tournament was *the* place to be seen. She'd bought her outfit weeks ago.

The man reached over and stroked her arm, and she resisted the urge to snatch it away. "Excellent. I look forward to seeing you there."

"I can't wait."

Her husband stepped forward and wrapped an arm around her waist. Once she'd have melted into him, grateful for his support, but now she felt nothing but contempt.

The man she'd once loved leaned down and kissed her temple, the touch of his lips a lie. She avoided the temptation to back away. It wouldn't look good in front of their so-called friends. How many of them knew what he'd done and didn't tell her?

"Need a top up?" the bastard asked.

"I'd better switch to water." It was her turn to drive.

She'd have to hold off on the vodka until she got home.

Her husband motioned to a waiter, and seconds later a hi-ball glass of sparkling water was placed into her hand. She gripped it tightly, wondering how hard she'd have to press before it shattered. Like her heart.

She gritted her teeth as another acquaintance appeared, shaking her husband's hand and leaning in to kiss her on both cheeks. Fake. Everyone in this room was fake. Except her. Susan was an open wound, pain leaking out like her lifeblood.

Nobody noticed.

"Ooh, Susie. It's been what, two weeks since we saw each other?" Her best friend rushed in with a hug.

Ex, Susan corrected herself. Her ex-best friend. And she was wrong. Susan saw her less than a week ago. Five days, twenty one hours and fourteen minutes ago to be precise. In her bedroom. Under her husband.

Of course, Loretta had her eyes closed and her head thrown back so she didn't notice Susan watching from the doorway. But Susan knew the truth now, and that image would stay with her forever, as clearly as if it happened yesterday.

Her first instinct had been to run from the house, but on the drive to her lawyer's office she came to her senses. Divorcing Jerome would mean losing the home she'd worked so hard to decorate, not to mention the country club membership she'd coveted so much when she worked her summers there serving drinks to the rich and famous.

Susan hadn't grown up wealthy. Her father was a mailman and her brother worked in an auto shop. As a little girl, she'd vowed not to turn into her mother, eking out the groceries to the end of the week and patching her clothes together. If she left Jerome, her social standing would take a serious hit.

No, there had to be a better solution. At thirty-five, Susan wasn't getting any younger. Starting over would be tough.

So she sucked it up. Literally, in Jerome's case, although she'd had to fight from gagging when she pictured where his cock had been the day before.

Susan forced a smile as Loretta hovered in front of her. "Too busy to come to the club?" she asked.

"We've had the interior designers in." Loretta shrugged. "You know how it goes. Anyway, how have you been?"

"I've had my own dramas. The spa mixed up my nail appointment last Monday. Can you believe that?" And if they hadn't, Susan would never have caught Loretta nailing her husband.

"They double booked my weekly massage last month as well. They really need to think about getting a new receptionist."

Jerome turned from whichever captain of industry he was talking to and stood next to Loretta. Too damn close. Susan felt her eyes narrow and forced herself to relax. Acting normal was the key.

Speaking of keys...

"Would you be a doll and get my phone out the car?"

Jerome dangled the car keys on his outstretched finger. "It's not in my pocket. I must have left it in the centre console. Or maybe the door pocket." Beside him, Loretta smiled encouragingly.

"Of course, honey." Susan resisted the urge to break a finger, and instead reached out and plucked the keys neatly from him. "Back in a jiffy."

As she walked away, Loretta's voice turned sickly sweet. "Jerome, have you seen the view across the valley from the back deck? It's to die for. You simply must let me show you."

The view? More like her tonsils. Jerome didn't need his phone, merely an excuse to be alone with Loretta. As Susan glanced behind, she saw the pair heading for the rear of the house and quickened her own steps.

The car keys dug into Susan's palm as she crunched across the gravel driveway on her navy blue stilettos. Why hadn't she noticed Jerome's betrayal sooner? She began to question every late business meeting, every out of town conference. How many of them had been real? And worse - was Loretta the first? Jerome seemed to go through one or two secretaries a year, each of them younger and prettier than the last. Were any of them providing additional services?

Sure, she'd heard of issues like this happening to other women, but she'd always been determined she wouldn't be one of them. For years she'd religiously plucked, waxed, vibrated and polished her way to a body that would pass for a decade younger. And this was how Jerome repaid her?

She seethed as she tripped over a stray statue in her stupid shoes. Those were another thing she hated, but Jerome stood six inches taller so she needed the extra height. Why did they have to park so far away? "Let's arrive fashionably late," Jerome said. That translated as missing the best canapés and having to walk half a mile to the Mercedes.

As Susan neared the vehicle, she saw Loretta's red convertible pulled in behind, the metallic paint gleaming in the moonlight. In an instant, her luck had changed.

Maybe this wouldn't be such a bad night after all.

***

The first fat drops of rain fell as Susan scurried back through the front door. Jerome and Loretta were already back in the house, looking cosy by the faux-fireplace.

Susan handed the phone over and Jerome tucked it away in his jacket pocket. See? He didn't even use it. "Thanks, sweetheart. Loretta's been telling me all about Jim's new yacht. They've invited us out for a sail. Isn't that terrific?"

"Fabulous." Although Jim having a new yacht wasn't terrible news. That meant Jerome would want one too, and Susan found the forty-footer they owned at the moment incredibly cramped. "Loretta, can I get you another glass of wine?"

She giggled. "Better not. This is my second already."

"Better safe than sorry."

Another hour of excruciating small talk followed, and the effort of having to be nice to Loretta gave Susan an awful migraine. She gulped a couple of paracetamol down and willed her churning stomach to still.

"You feeling all right, sweetheart?" Jerome asked. "We could head off now?"

Since Loretta headed off five minutes ago, citing an early start, he'd lost interest in the party.

"If you don't mind. I could do with some rest." She rubbed her temples for effect. "This music's given me a headache."

Jerome steered her round the room as they said their goodbyes, the touch of his hand on the bare skin at her lower back making her flesh crawl. By the time they escaped, the rain was hammering down. On a normal night, Susan would have been upset by the thought of getting wet, but tonight was no normal night.

She couldn't help smiling heavenwards, a silent thanks for the rain sent to wash away the evidence.

"Sure you're okay to drive?" Jerome asked, as they reached the car. "We could ring for a cab."

"I'm fine. Really."

Susan carefully belted herself in and started the engine. As she pulled away, gently accelerating down the hill, the rain seemed to fall even harder. If she hadn't been looking for it, she'd have easily missed the dark gap in the railings at the end of the road. She slowed up for the hairpin, not wanting to go the same way as Loretta.

Careful to maintain a blank facade, she gave herself a mental high five. All those boring hours spent helping her brother to fix his car as a teenager had finally paid off. Susan knew exactly which spot on Loretta's front brake lines to cut with the penknife Jerome insisted on keeping in the glove compartment.

Susan's only regret was that she hadn't been there to hear Loretta scream as she sailed over the edge.

Still, that couldn't be helped. She put it out of her mind as she thought ahead to her next problem - what to do about the man sitting next to her...

THE OFFICE

THE INTERCOM BUZZED for the fifth time that hour. Yes, Helen was counting. It was a little game she played with herself to break up the day, although Mr. Deakins had some way to go before he beat his record from one memorable Thursday last year. Seventy two buzzes. She had nightmares about it for weeks afterwards.

"Yes, Mr. Deakins."

Eleven years she'd worked for him, and he still insisted she use his title. What did one have to do to be allowed to call him John? She stifled a giggle as she imagined his sour-faced ex-wife in bed with him, crying, "Oh, yes, Mr. Deakins!"

"Could you come through? I need you to take a letter."

Other managers at the company typed letters themselves, but Mr. Deakins liked to pace his office as he dictated, leaving Helen to frantically scribble down his words in shorthand.

He hadn't been quite so difficult when she first started, but as times had moved on he'd remained set in his ways. He'd become even more obnoxious after his wife ran off with the window cleaner four years ago. A lucky escape, that's what Helen called it.

She'd long dreamed of meeting her own window cleaner, but with the fourteen hour days she worked, six days a week, she barely had time to look out her grimy windows let alone arrange to get them cleaned.

Picturing Mr. Deakins' face growing redder by the second, Helen snatched up her notepad and hurried into the inner sanctum.

***

An hour later, Helen sat at her computer, translating her notes into text on the screen. The process was never easy--Mr. Deakins kept changing his mind about what he wanted to say, leaving every draft with more crossed out than left in. Still, she was used to it now.

She'd barely got a quarter of the way through when the intercom buzzed again. "Did you collect my dry cleaning?"

"It's hanging on the back of your door."

"Ah. Would you be a dear and pop out to the supermarket? I forgot to pick up dinner."

Couldn't be bothered, more like. He "forgot" something at least three times a week. Helen spent more time doing his shopping than her own. And it wasn't just groceries--clothes, furniture, birthday gifts and household goods, she purchased them all.

She forced a smile onto her face. One of those soft skills courses she went on said people knew whether you were smiling, even if they couldn't see your face, and she always liked to sound cheerful even if she didn't feel it.

"Is there anything in particular you'd like to eat?"

He chuckled. "Oh, you know me. Just get something nice."

He said that every time, then moaned about her choices when she took in his first cup of tea the next morning. Every day. Without fail.

But what could she do? He was the boss and she was paid to do as she was to, even if his requests went way beyond her remit. She'd once considered complaining to HR about the extra work, but immediately dismissed the idea. Mr. Deakins played golf with the HR manager, so it was easy to guess whose side he'd be on.

Helen snatched a twenty pound note from the float Mr. Deakins left in her desk drawer and left for Tesco. It was raining once again, par for the course in a British summer. She longed for fluffy clouds drifting across a blue sky, and the lap of waves on a sandy beach. One day, she promised herself, one day.

"Back again?" the checkout lady asked as Helen stacked up a brie and cranberry wellington, a portion of ready-mashed potato and a bottle of red wine on the conveyor belt.

"As always."

"That's a nice wine. I tried it myself last week."

"I'm sure it's lovely." Mr. Deakins could guzzle Cristal and still moan about the taste.

"Eleven pounds and seventeen pence."

Helen handed over the money, careful to get a receipt. Mr. Deakins went through them every Friday to check she hadn't short changed him. In all the time she'd worked for him the receipts never came in a penny short, but he still insisted on doing it. "Always pays to be careful," he said.

As she stowed his food in the fridge in the kitchen, one of the other secretaries popped in.

"Has the old bastard sent you out on his personal errands again?"

Helen shrugged. "Nothing changes."

The other girl shuddered. "I couldn't put up with being treated like that. Shelley said he made you take his urine sample into the doctor's last week?"

"I'd rather forget about that." Helen scrubbed her hands a dozen times after she got back, and just thinking about it now gave her the urge to rush to the bathroom again.

"Why do you stay?"

"I'm used to it."

That wasn't entirely true. Helen would never get used to Mr. Deakins and his obnoxious ways. It was more that she didn't know anything else. She came to work for Fraser & Co right from school, and now at age fifty-five, she didn't know how to do anything different. And all her other bosses had been pleasant. It was just Mr. Deakins' funeral she dreamed of attending.

A couple of years ago, she'd been on the verge of saying "to hell with it" and handing in her notice anyway, but after carefully weighing up her options, she'd decided to stick it out until her retirement. After all, that wasn't so far away now.

It wasn't long before Mr. Deakins headed off for the evening, leaving Helen with a stack of brochures to send out, a business trip to arrange and a conference room to set up for first thing the next morning. She didn't crawl into her own flat until almost nine. What was the point in going home?

Once upon a time, her cat, Snoopy, would have been on the doorstep to welcome her home, but he'd passed on last year at the grand old age of seventeen.

She'd toyed with the idea of getting another companion, but decided to hold out until she had more time to devote to a pet. Animals needed love too.

**

The next morning, Helen was at her desk bright and early. The conference started at ten, and Mr. Deakins had important things to do beforehand, which meant Helen needed to organise them.

At quarter to ten, the intercom buzzed. "What else have I got left to do?"

"Just the authorisation for the weekly payment run, Mr. Deakins."

He gutted at the other end. "Well, hurry up and bring it in then. Is lunch organised?"

"Yes, Mr. Deakins."

As she had every Wednesday for the last nine years, Helen carried the folder of invoices in and placed them on his desk. He fished his reading glasses out and balanced them on the end of his nose.

"Big run this week," he said.

Her heart beat faster as he scanned down the list of amounts. "The final balance is due on the factory extension and we need to pay for raw materials for the new China contract. That's what accounts said."

"Ah, yes." He logged on to the banking system and authorised the transfers just as his first guests arrived.

Helen breathed a sigh of relief as he left his office. Thank goodness that was over. She hugged the folder to her chest as she scurried back to her desk, ready to tackle the next job on her list. Filing.

Her gaze lingered on the two largest invoices as she

sorted the pile into alphabetical order. Seven hundred thousand pounds between the pair. She couldn't help but be proud of them. It took her ages to get the logos just right, but all the practice she'd had creating documents for Mr. Deakins finally paid off. They were indistinguishable from the originals, apart from the bank details of course.

Helen thought the next part would be easy, but it turned out to be the most nerve-racking experience of her life. And after working for Mr. Deakins for almost a decade, that wasn't a statement she made lightly.

The bank clearing system worked on a three day cycle, which meant she had to wait until Friday to collect her cash. In that little she had of her evenings, she busied herself with packing, although there was little from her old life she wanted to take with her. There wasn't much call for woolly jumpers and snow boots in Panama.

***

The money arrived early on Friday. When she logged on for the fourth time, there it was. Her freedom. Her retirement fund. She was tempting to walk straight out the building and catch a cab to the airport, but she was nothing of not patient. She'd wait it out. No point in arousing suspicions unnecessarily. Besides, she still had Mr. Deakins' shopping to do.

"What have you got me today?" he asked when she handed the grocery bag over.

"Lamb curry, Mr. Deakins. With rice and naan bread." And a garnish of ricin. She'd grown the castor oil beans herself and extracted the deadly poison according to a recipe she found on the internet. The process had been surprisingly easy, and the plants were pretty, too. She'd been a keen gardener back when she'd had more time to herself. She couldn't wait to start growing her own fruit again.

Mr Deakins wrinkled his nose. "Let's hope it tastes better than the beef abomination you fetched me last week."

She smiled brightly, her mind already on the journey ahead. Her flight to Manila left in four hours. "Who knows? Maybe you'll get an interesting surprise."

CREEP

"HE'S TALKING BULLSHIT. He doesn't care what grades we get."

"Yeah." Mike agreed with Joe. Mr. Smart was on a power trip for sure. The bastard got a kick out of putting them in detention. And for what? All they did was pass a note. So it was about the asshole's wife - he should have been flattered they thought she was hot.

"And we've missed football practice."

"Yeah." Mike was a boy of few words, but his tone said it all. Missing practice hacked him right off. He'd never make the team if he didn't impress the coach, and skipping a session so he could sit in the biology lab copying out pages from the textbook wasn't the way to do it.

"How would he like it?" Joe asked. "What would he say if he missed something really important because of some dickhead?"

Joe had an idea, and his lips curled slowly into a smile. "Why don't we find out?"

"What do you mean?"

"We know where he lives, right?"

Joe picked up on his train of thought. "Didn't he move into the old Woodrow house on the edge of town? We could go round there and... and... do something."

"That's the place. My uncle said they completely

renovated it from the basement up. Let's go there and let the air out of his tyres. Make him late for a change."

"Tonight?"

"Why not? You busy?" The way he said it, "busy" meant "chicken."

"No way! I'm in." Joe's voice wavered a little, in contrast to his words.

Mike chuckled. He enjoyed scaring his friend from time to time, but it was good for him, right? Face your fears and all that. "Meet me outside my house at nine."

***

"Ready to go?" Mike asked Joe.

His head bobbed up and down and he swallowed. "Yep."

Like Mike, Joe had come dressed in black. Good. Mike didn't want to be seen as they snuck into the driveway. Getting caught doing something they shouldn't once that day was quite enough. Mr. Smart would probably call the cops if he saw them.

The old Woodrow place was over a mile away and they set off in silence, keeping to the shadows. A neighbour's dog leapt at the fence as they walked past, barking, and Mike almost stumbled off the kerb. He looked round at Joe, hoping he hadn't seen him jump, but the smaller boy was ten feet back, his face white in the dim glow from a streetlight.

"Hurry up, don't be scared. He can't get you." Mike took a step closer to the fence, and the animal hurled itself against the wooden boards again.

"I-I-I know." Joe scurried to catch up, sticking close to Mike as they half-ran down the road.

The dog's growls faded as they turned into the next street. The houses grew larger, further apart, and the darkness grew more intense as the streetlights petered out, leaving only the moon to guide them.

"Did you bring a torch?" Joe asked.

"Yeah, but I don't wanna turn it on unless we have to." No point in announcing their arrival.

"Maybe we can use it on the way back?"

"Yeah, maybe."

They were almost at the house now, and Mike slowed his steps. His heart did the opposite, beating faster and faster until it seemed as if the whole neighbourhood would hear. A tree behind rustled as Joe brushed against it, and Mike turned and put a finger to his lips. He usually went on these sort of jaunts alone, but having Mike along gave his ego a boost. Let him learn from the master.

Plus if they did get caught, Mike could say it was all Joe's idea.

The drive was gravelled, but luckily a lawn ran alongside. Mike crept across the stones on tiptoe, breathing a sigh of relief as his feet touched grass. Joe did the same, and crouched beside him as he studied the sprawling bungalow. Only two lights were visible - the glow in the hallway, mottled through the privacy glass next to the front door, and a chink of light shining through the gap in the curtains to the right.

"Reckon that's the lounge?" he asked Joe.

"Probably. I doubt it's the kitchen, not at the front of the house like that."

"Looks as if his wife's home." Two cars sat in the driveway. Mr. Smart's Chevrolet was nearest, a dull grey, just like its owner. Beyond it sat Mrs. Smart's sporty red Mazda. How the old man pulled a fit bird like her mystified Mike. It wasn't as if he was rich or anything. How much did a biology teacher make? Thirty grand? Forty? And some dude in the year above reckoned Smart's wife was a doctor. She must earn a bomb. No, there must be other attraction but Mike couldn't fathom what it might be.

"So we're gonna let the air out his tyres, right?" Joe asked.

Mike pulled the pen knife his uncle gave him for Christmas out of his pocket and snapped the blade open. "I think we can do a little better than that."

Joe's eyes widened in the moonlight. "Are you serious?"

Mike made quiet clucking noises and Joe looked away.

"I mean, yeah, sounds like a good idea."

It wasn't the first time Mike had slashed a tyre. In fact, he'd made it something of an art form. Thirteen cars in the last year alone, some belonging to people who'd pissed him off, the rest to strangers to throw the cops off the scent.

He knew just the right spot to stab to penetrate the sidewall, and the hiss as air escaped always put a smile on his face. The local paper even gave him a nickname - The Silent Slasher. Had a nice ring to it.

Two tyres down, two to go. Should he go for the wife's car as well?

"Hurry up!" Joe whispered.

"Just another minute." Mike got to work on the third tyre, and the car settled lower on the damp driveway.

Four done. Mike glanced over at the house,

considering his options. Mrs. Smart had never done anything to hurt him, but then again, she was married to an asshole and that made her the enemy. As he took a step closer to the Madza, another light flicked on at the side of the house.

He paused, and the lady herself walked past wearing a tight vest top. Nice. Abandoning thoughts of the car, he walked slowly towards the house.

"Where are you going?" Joe asked. He didn't bother to hide his fear that time.

"Just getting a closer look. Shame she's dressed."

"We should go. What if my parents notice I'm gone?"

"You're fifteen. I can't believe you still have a curfew." Mike's own father gave up caring long ago, and he couldn't even remember what his mother looked like. Now, where did the woman go? Would she come back? It want every day Mike got to see a real, live Barbie doll.

He snuck closer to the window, and Joe followed. Mike knew he wouldn't stay behind. The kid was scared of his own shadow.

Mike got near enough for his breath to mist on the window, then drew back a foot. He didn't want to get spotted. As long as he didn't squash his face up to the window, he figured it would be difficult for someone looking out into the dark to see him.

He tucked his knife back in his pocket and adjusted his pants. The evening's excitement had quite an effect on him. Now, he just needed the hot wife to come back.

The bush rustled behind him, and he turned round to shush Joe. Next time, he was leaving him behind. "Will you..."

His mouth dropped open as Mr. Smart's arm tightened around Joe's neck. Joe was silent, but the wet patch on the front of his pants gave a good indication of how he was feeling.

"What the...?"

Mr. Smart smiled, the happiest Mike had ever seen him look. "If it isn't my two favourite pupils. What an unexpected surprise. Didn't you get enough of me this afternoon?"

"Let him go." Mike found his tongue and the words tumbled out. "He can't breathe." Teachers weren't supposed to choke their pupils. Didn't they have to take an oath to look after them or something?

Mr. Smart's grin grew wider. "That's the whole idea."

For the first time, Mike felt genuine fear creep up his spine. Up until then, adrenalin had given him bravado, but now it seeped away. "Let him go," he said again, but without same force.

Mr. Smart chuckled, only nothing was funny. "Are you gonna make me?"

In his drab, grey suits, Mr. Smart looked like a geek, but wearing just a T-shirt, Mike saw the muscles bulging in his arms. He couldn't match that. Joe's eyelids were drooping as he lost consciousness, so he'd be no help.

Mike needed to act, but how? Then it came to him. The knife! He reached into his pocket and came out with the blade. There was a satisfying snnnnick as it popped open. He loved that sound.

"You think you're the big guy, huh?" Mike lowered the blade to charge, but screamed in agony instead as his arm was twisted behind him. The scream that left his lips drowned out the sound of his bone snapping.

Mr. Smart's teeth glinted in the moonlight. "Oh no. I'd never think that. I know who wears the trousers in my relationship."

A searing pain shot through Mike's back as he landed in the dirt. Blinking away tears, he stared up at Mrs. Smart. The Barbie doll. She pressed a foot over his windpipe as he sucked in air. Whatever she'd done to him meant his arms didn't work. He tried to lift one, but only got a few inches before it flopped back on the dirt.

She grinned, teeth bright in the gloom. A killer smile.

But her eyes were ice. They softened a little as she gazed at her husband. "Honey, you realise if we keep doing this, we'll have to move again?"

"Doing what?" Mike gasped.

She looked down at him, her face a mask of irritation, then spoke as if he was ten years younger. "When we were at university, we discovered the best way to learn about human anatomy was to explore it for ourselves. It's what makes us so good at our jobs."

"It's a labour of love," Mr. Smart added. "We've spent many happy hours studying our specimens."

Mike got an eyeful of Mrs. Smart's chest as she stooped to pick up his knife, but it no longer held the same fascination. He longed to be back in his room, fighting for floor space with his little brother. As he stared up at the face of a monster, he made a promise to himself: If he got out of this, he'd never disobey a teacher again. Or snoop on other people's property. Or vandalise cars. Or...

It was a promise he never got to keep.

NOTHING BEATS A GOOD COFFEE

"MORNING, DAPHNE. YOUR usual?"

She smiled. The name on her birth certificate was something else entirely, but Daphne worked. "Yes, please."

Rosario stepped back and picked up a tall cup, then turned to the coffee machine.

Daphne's mouth began to water. Nobody made her latte with caramel drizzle the way Rosario did. Too much milk, not enough milk - there was always something wrong. And don't even get her started on the caramel. From Dublin to Delhi, she'd tried coffee shops the world over, but Rosario had every barista beaten hands down.

She'd stumbled across the tiny cafe three years ago, tucked away on a side street, and now she visited every day she was in town. Rosario always had a smile and a kind word, and for her that was important. In her line of work, friends were hard to come by. It was all too easy to get stabbed in the back.

The cafe gave her a home from home, a place to while away an hour with the illusion of normality. A few others did the same. The lady who always took the corner seat at the back, choosing to start her day in public but ignoring the world around her. The man sitting on the couch by the door, reading the paper.

Daphne saw him at least three times a week. She'd got curious once and followed him when he left, going via his mistress's apartment to the smart oceanfront home he shared with his uptight wife.

Everybody had a secret.

A new face walked up to the counter, a businessman in a tailored suit. He eyed up the pastries in the cabinet before ordering a non-fat flat white. Figured. He probably never let himself had any fun.

Mind you, Daphne rarely had time for that, either. At the peak of her profession, she needed to strike while the iron was hot if she was to meet her goal of retiring at thirty. Two more years to go. Her bank account grew fatter every month, and the thought of spending her later years relaxing on the beach kept her going. That and Rosario's coffee.

Another customer ran in, a teenager wanting a cookie, and Rosario paused to serve him while the coffee machine hissed and gurgled in the background. Daphne waited patiently as the businessman and kid disappeared out the door, watching as Rosario drew a zigzag pattern on the froth of her drink in caramel.

"Do you want a blueberry muffin today?"

Ah yes, her other weakness. Was today a muffin day? She thought so, yes. She'd worked damned hard this week, and just when she thought she'd get a day off, an unexpected job came up. Unexpected, but oh-so-necessary. Completing it took her most of the previous night, and she stifled a yawn as she nodded. "Yes, please."

Rosario carefully placed her treat onto a plate and added a napkin and one of those tiny little sugar cookies. Then he winked at her and added another. She couldn't help giggling in return as she passed a ten dollar bill over.

"Keep the change."

It was Rosario's turn to grin. "You always pay too much."

"Your coffee's worth it."

"I wish everyone thought the same."

"Ah yes, how are things with the dragon?"

Rosario picked up Daphne's cup and plate and carried them over to the table she always sat at. Back to the wall, facing the window. She settled into her seat and Rosario plopped onto a stool opposite.

He let out a long sigh. "She yelled at me six times yesterday. I wrote my resignation letter out last night ready to hand in, but she's not here yet. If I turn up a second late, she chews me out but she should have arrived an hour ago and I haven't had so much as a phone call."

"Some people are damned inconsiderate, hey?"

"Yeah, but I can't complain too much. I'd rather she wasn't here." He watched Daphne from under his eyelashes. "It means I can stop and talk with you for a few minutes."

See? Rosario always managed to boost her ego. Even her ex-husband had struggled to do that. She sipped her latte and pushed the man out of her mind. Her time with him had been a valuable learning experience, but not one she cared to repeat.

"Maybe she won't come in at all?" Daphne suggested.

"Every night for the past year I've said a little prayer that she'll quit, but nobody's answered it. I doubt today's any different."

But it was. He didn't know it yet, but it was. Daphne peeled down the wrapper on her muffin and took a bite. "There's always somebody listening."

The bell over the door sounded and Rosario jumped up, relaxing when he saw another customer rather than the supervisor he hated so much.

"I need to serve this lady. Maybe you'll still be around a bit later?"

Daphne nodded and smiled. She could manage that.

As she sipped her coffee, she stared out the window at the people walking past. They fascinated her, people. How they walked, how they talked. How they lived, how they died. The blood-stained knife she'd used that morning still lay in her handbag, covered with her blue silk scarf. She'd get rid of it later, but she needed her coffee-and-Rosario fix first.

After all, he was the reason it was there in the first place.

With the bitch's bluster and bravado at the coffee shop, when she shouted at poor Rosario for every transgression, real or imagined, Daphne had been expecting a struggle when she killed her. But the dragon stayed silent as Daphne slid the paring knife between her fifth and sixth ribs. Barely a whimper. Of course, Daphne had her in a well-practised choke hold, but even so, it was almost disappointing.

Daphne popped a stray blueberry into her mouth and chided herself - she really shouldn't think like that. Easy jobs were the best ones although she secretly liked a bit of excitement. Like the assassination she'd carried out in Mexico earlier in the week. Now, that had been entertaining.

A silenced bullet, a chase across rooftops, escape on a motorcycle, all with her as the star - a real James Bond moment. She'd even caught herself humming the theme tune as she zoomed up the coast in a speedboat. Happy days.

She shook her head infinitesimally as an old man rode past on a motorised cart. She'd sure miss the thrills when she quit, but if she carried on too long she'd end up in a bodybag herself. Contract killing was one of those industries where the operators had a short lifespan.

Normally she charged top dollar, but last night's job had been a freebie. Nobody came between a woman and her coffee, and the dragon lady should have remembered that. She should also have remembered to be nice to people. Somebody always noticed if you weren't.

Daphne had almost reached the bottom of her cup when Rosario came to sit with her again. He slid a fresh drink across to her, averting his eyes as he did so.

"It's on the house. I thought you might still be thirsty."

She eyed up the size of the first cup. Any bigger and she'd need a second bladder. "Really?"

He gave her a shy smile. "Okay, so I was creating a reason for you to stay a bit longer."

A delicious shiver ran through her as Rosario shuffled his stool closer. Men rarely gave her a second glance and usually that was a good thing. Her hair was mousey, her face plain, and that let her blend into the background. Nobody ever suspected her. But sometimes, just sometimes, she wished...

"...what do you say?"

"Sorry, what?" She shouldn't zone out like that. It could be dangerous.

"I was just wondering if you wanted to have dinner with me."

All of a sudden, it was as if he'd thrown a bucket of cold water over her. Not a date. She didn't date. Relationships simply weren't compatible with her occupation. That was one of the lessons her husband taught her almost a decade ago. She'd had to be incredibly careful when she disposed of his body.

"I'm in a relationship at the moment." A threesome, with her gun and her knife. It was the easiest excuse to use. "But it's good to be friends."

"Friends." Rosario reached over and squeezed her hand, his fingers warm around hers. "Everybody can use extra friends."

She squeezed back, glad she'd worn gloves earlier so she didn't get blood under her fingernails. That was always a bitch to get out. "You're right there."

With one last quirk of his lips, he got up. She watched him walk back to the counter, admiring his taut ass. Who knew? Maybe in a couple of years when things were different she'd be able to accept his invitation? Life sometimes took an unexpected course. She'd proved that earlier.

In the meantime, she'd be back whenever she could to enjoy her latte with caramel drizzle and a little taste of Rosario...

THANK YOU FOR READING

FOR AN AUTHOR, every review is incredibly important. Not only do they make writers feel warm and fuzzy inside, readers consider them when making their decision whether or not to buy a book.

If you enjoyed Twisted, it would be amazing if you took a few minutes to let the rest of the world know. Even a line saying you enjoyed the book, or what your favourite part was, helps a lot.

Better still, if you write a review for this book and email Elise a link to it at elise@elise-noble.com, she'll send you a free copy of Pitch Black.

What's **Pitch Black** about?

Even a Diamond can be shattered...

After the owner of a security company is murdered, his sharp-edged wife goes on the run. Forced to abandon everything she holds dear - her home, her friends, her job in special ops - she builds a new life for herself in England. As Ashlyn Hale, she meets Luke, a handsome local who makes her realise just how lonely she is.

Yet, even in the sleepy village of Lower Foxford, the

dark side of life dogs Diamond's trail when the unthinkable strikes. Forced out of hiding, she races against time to save those she cares about. But is it too little, too late?

WARNING
If you want sweetness and light and all things bright,
Diamond's not the girl for you.
She's got sass, she's got snark, and she's bitchy and dark,
As she does what a girl's got to do.